MW00594131

From:

The Night Before Christmas dot.com

By Claudine Gandolfi

Illustrated and designed by Kerren Barbas

 PETER PAUPER PRESS, INC.
White Plains, New York

Illustrations copyright © 2001
Kerren Barbas

Text copyright © 2001
Peter Pauper Press, Inc.
202 Mamaroneck Avenue
White Plains, NY 10601
ISBN 0-88088-844-X
Printed in China
7 6 5 4 3 2 1

Visit us at www.peterpauper.com

The Night Before Christmas dot.com

'Twas the
night before
Christmas,
when all through
the house

My hard drive
was *purring*
alongside my
mouse.

The sites were all bookmarked,

my

passwords

all saved,

In hopes that the mall rush

need NEVER be braved.

The children

pretended

to sleep, though

not tired,

While millions of eToys were what they desired;

And Mamma

on her PC,

and I on

my Mac,

Had quickly
logged on for a
shopping
attack.

When right
on my
screen
there
arose a
commotion,

I knew
that I'd
miss the

free shipping

promotion!

Off to my
handbook I flew
like a flash,

Tore open the
pages, and read,

SYSTEM CRASH.

The monitor
gave off a
crestfallen
GLOW

As I banged at the keyboard

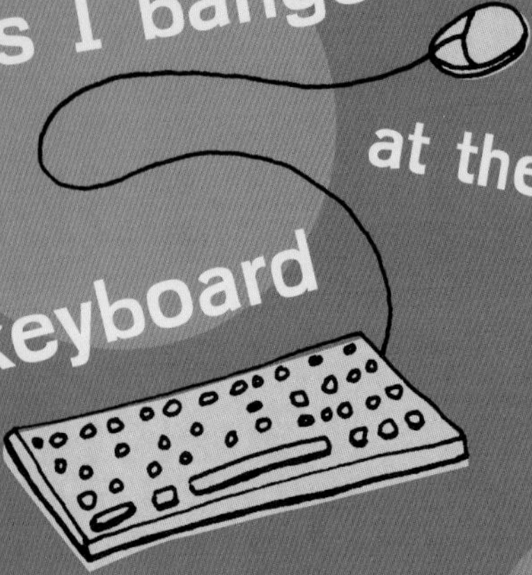

and whimpered,

"Oh, no!"

When,
what to my eyes
did appear
with a start,

But a red
Christmas
sleigh and a big
shopping cart.

With a little eShopper,

**so nimble
and quick,**

I knew
in an instant
it must be

More rapid
than modems,
he began to
explore

And laughed
as he went
from eStore
to eStore.

games

"To the toy site!

shopping

bidding

To the
auction!

And now for CDs!

I've found
some great
bargains that
surely will
please:

Hot gadgets!

Best-sellers!

A new bat

and ball!

Now ship today!

Ship today!

Ship today all!"

As the

dry leaves

that on my new

Screensaver

fly,

When they

meet with some

movement,

all vanish

(Good-bye!),

Away
with each
mouse-click
my Net
worries flew,

Replaced
by the cart
for St. Click
to review.

And then,
in an instant,

I heard
on my
speakers,

You've got mail!

—a receipt
for that new pair
of sneakers!

As I drew
back my hand
and deleted
my cache,

Through my
desktop
St. Clickolas leapt
with a flash.

He was
dressed all
in fleece,

from his head to his toes,

And wore
slippers that
matched all his
comfortable
clothes.

A shiny
new laptop
was perched on
his hip,

And he carried his data

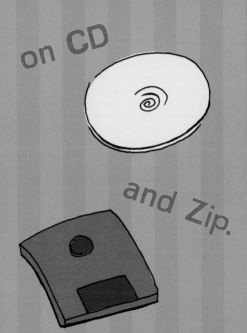

on CD

and Zip.

His eyes were
quite bleary;
his wrists
somewhat tender.

His bottom,
from sitting,
had grown much
less slender!

His dimples
and mouth
wore a
holiday grin

That
brightened his
face and the
beard
on his chin.

His well-designed mouse had a form-fitting shape,

And his fingers reached all the keys, even "Escape"!

His laptop
was loaded
and scanned free
of virus,

His
software,
updated—how
very desirous!

He was
cuddly
and cute,
a right jolly
old sprite,

And he
showed me
that shopping
can be
a delight.

A wink
of his eye
after credit
inspection

Soon gave
me to know
I had buyer's
protection!

**He spoke
not a word but
stared straight
at the screen**

And purchased
all presents
for toddler
through teen,

And clicking

his thumb

on the side

of his mouse,

Jumped back through my screen and vacated my house;

He sprang
to his sleigh,
with a wave
did depart . . .

"Oh,
thank you!"

I shouted,

with
all
of
my
heart.

And I
heard him
exclaim,

as I
logged
off the site,

"Merry Christmas
to all, and to all
a good night!"